Arax
The Soul Stealer

BY ADAM BLADE

ORCHARD

THE ICY PLAINS

THE NORTHERN MOUNTAINS

THE CENTRAL PLAINS

WESTERN OCEAN

THE FOREST OF FEAR

GRASSY PLAINS

KI HU DA

THE WINDING RIVER

THE RUBY DESERT

SPINDREL

Beasts of Avantia

THE PIT OF FIRE

MALVEL'S MAZE

STONEWIN VOLCANO

...CITY

ERRINEL

THE DEAD VALLEY

THE DEAD JUNGLE

THE DARK WOOD

THE DARK JUNGLE

CONTENTS

STORY ONE

A FRIEND LOST

I am Marc, apprentice to the good wizard Aduro. My master is in danger. The evil wizard Malvel has cast a powerful spell on him. Brave Tom now faces his greatest challenge yet. Can he save his friend Aduro and protect the kingdom of Avantia?

Chapter 1
THE SILENT PALACE

Tom and Elenna were staying at the Palace as guests of King Hugo. Sunshine streamed through the windows as the friends ran downstairs. Then Tom stopped. "What can you hear, Elenna?" he asked.

"Nothing," she replied. "It's really quiet."

"Exactly," said Tom. "We haven't even seen a servant."

The Great Hall lay silent.
The king's throne was empty.
No fire had been lit.

"It's really spooky," agreed
Elenna. Then a guard burst in.

"You there," he said. "I
have orders from the king. You
must go to the wizard Aduro's
chambers straight away."

"Where is everyone?" asked Elenna.

"They are in their rooms, by order of the king. The Palace is not safe," replied the guard.

Tom and Elenna ran up the spiral staircase that led to Aduro's private rooms. The wooden door glowed strangely around the edges.

Inside, the friends found a man with wild eyes, hissing and growling. He was being closely watched by guards.

The man was their old friend,

the good wizard Aduro himself.

Tom stared in horror. Aduro's
face, usually filled with kindness,
was instead twisted in anger.

Suddenly, the old wizard leapt
up, jabbing Tom with his finger.

"Evil Malvel must have done
this to Aduro!" Tom said.
Marc, the apprentice,
muttered some words and
an image of a giant creature

formed in the air. It had a horned head and wings like a bat. It was hitting Aduro with a whip of thorns which tore into his heart. Aduro cried out and a look of evil replaced the kindness in his eyes.

As the vision disappeared, King Hugo said sadly, "The Beast has stolen Aduro's soul, and left this behind." The king showed them a scrap of material stained with blood.

"My name is sewn into it!" Tom said, frightened.

King Hugo stared into Tom's eyes. "I am going to send you on a Quest. You will need to be strong and brave. Malvel's new Beast must be found before more damage is caused to our kingdom."

"You can count on me," declared Tom. Elenna agreed.

"Take great care and fight bravely. Avantia depends on you," finished the king.

Chapter 2
A NEW QUEST!

As they ran off, Tom heard a whisper in his head. "Arax the Soul Stealer will find you!" it said. The voice was Malvel's.

Tom and Elenna ran to the stables to find their faithful friends. Tom unlatched the door and saddled Storm, his black stallion, ready for the journey. Meanwhile Silver, Elenna's pet wolf, dashed around, barking with excitement.

"Where do we find this new Beast?" asked Elenna. "He could be anywhere."

"My map will tell us," said Tom. He began to open it and then suddenly stopped. He

looked worried. "Aduro gave this map to me," he said. "Will it be any use to us, without his good magic?"

"There's only one way to find out," Elenna told him.

Together, they unrolled the map
and laid it out. The parchment
looked blank. Then to Tom's relief,
a picture of Avantia appeared.
"Yes!" he exclaimed. "The map's

magic is still working."

"Then it must show Arax," said Elenna, kneeling at his side.

"Look!" cried Tom suddenly. "That's him!"

The two friends watched the tiny shape of Arax circle the mountaintops, then swoop down and vanish into the rock.

"We should have guessed that's where he'd be," said Elenna. "Arax is a bat – and bats live in caves!"

"Let's go!" said Tom, scrambling to his feet.

Tom leapt onto Storm's back
and Elenna jumped up behind
him. Soon they were out of the
city and heading west, with
the brave wolf Silver bounding
along beside them.

They rode for hours and by late afternoon the flat ground had given way to rocky slopes. They could see the mountains in the distance.

Storm had dropped to a slow trot, the loose rocks slippery under his hooves.

Tom could hear a faint rushing sound. "We must have reached the Winding River!" he said. "Let's set up camp here."

After a meal of berries and bread, they lay down to sleep.

Chapter 3
TO THE MOUNTAIN

Tom opened his eyes next morning to blue skies and warm sun. "Breakfast is served," joked Elenna, passing him a handful of nuts and berries.

When they had eaten, Tom got out his map and scanned the tall peaks. A tiny dark shape appeared on the map and then vanished again into a hole in the side of a mountain.

"That must be Arax's cave!" said Elenna. "But how do we get to it?"

"There must be a path," replied Tom, jumping up into Storm's saddle. "Come on!" Elenna leapt up behind him.

It wasn't long before they reached the start of the trail, the mountain peaks high above them. Silver followed Storm closely as the stallion picked his way over the sharp

rocks of the narrow path. The route soon became steep.

"We're climbing fast," said Elenna. "It's colder already."

Eventually the path became so difficult for Storm, Tom and Elenna jumped from the saddle. The four friends slowly struggled up the path together.

The sky was getting darker as they listened to the stream pounding over the rocks and great flocks of birds swooping and calling around the mountain tops.

"It's spooky here," muttered Elenna. "Do you think we're getting close to Arax's cave?"

Tom looked around at the bare grey rock dotted with scrubby bushes. "There's a dark cave there," he exclaimed. "Just like the one on the map!"

As they struggled towards the mouth of the cave, Elenna stopped. "I saw something!" she gasped.

A horrible hissing sound filled the air, and before Tom could do anything, a long

whip shot out of the cave and
wrapped itself around Elenna.
Tom jumped towards her, but it
was too late.

Elenna was dragged into
the dark cave and disappeared
among the shadows.

Tom recognised the whip from the vision Marc had shown them. Arax had taken Elenna! "Stay here," he ordered the animals as he crept into the cave. Where could Elenna be?

Chapter 4

THE GIANT BAT

Inside the cave, the air was suddenly filled with high-

pitched squeaks. A cloud of bats
whirled around Tom. He tried
to swipe at the creatures with
his sword but there were too
many of them. Their clawed
feet scratched his face and their
wings slapped against his skin.

The evil bats swooped and
dived. At last they tore out of
the cave and Tom was alone
again. He had to find Elenna.
After a while, Tom realised
he could hear the sound of
running water. His heart
was pounding as at last he
came across a huge waterfall
stretching across his path.
He took a deep breath and
plunged in, taking careful steps
until he was through.

Tom's face streamed with
water but when his vision

cleared, he saw Elenna, her
face pale. A creature with huge
claws grasped her round the
throat. It was Arax!

The Beast took hold of the spiked whip in one clawed hand. Tom felt sick knowing that the giant bat's whip could strike him at any time. He could see that Elenna was not hurt. Arax had been using her as bait to lure him into the cave.

As Tom charged forward the Beast was distracted for a few seconds and Elenna just managed to pull herself free. Arax flew at Tom, swirling his whip around. Faster and faster

it went until, with an almighty
crack, it ripped through his
tunic. Tom cried out as the
spikes bit into his flesh.

The giant bat pulled the whip back and began to whirl it around again. As the evil whip twisted, a shadowy figure began to appear which grew bigger. Then the bat Beast, Arax, shrieked in triumph and vanished into the cave leaving the shadowy figure in front of the children. Tom and Elenna gazed at the figure as it became more solid. It wasn't a huge Beast. It was only a boy who looked just like Tom.

"He looks like me," said Tom.

"No; his eyes are nothing like yours," said Elenna. "They're pure evil."

"My name is Nemico," snarled the boy. "You've met your match at last."

STORY TWO

RETURN OF A HERO

Once Aduro felt the bite of Arax's whip his soul was taken. Now he is a danger to himself and to Avantia. Can Tom and Elenna defeat the Beast, or will they meet the same terrible fate?

Chapter 1
ELENNA IN DANGER

"We're the same," Nemico told Tom. "But one fights for good, and the other for evil!"

Elenna took her chance and slipped safely out of the cave.

Desperate to follow her, Tom sliced his sword down through the air towards Nemico again and again until, at last, he drove the evil boy out onto the narrow mountain path. As Tom

lunged hard with his sword, an
arrow from Elenna flew past
Nemico's head.

"Foolish girl," Nemico
muttered. He took his shield
and sent it spinning through the
air, straight at her head.

The shield slammed into Elenna's head with a horrible thud.

"Elenna!" Tom gasped. "Are you all right?"

As his friend slowly got to her feet, Tom felt sick with relief.

"He won't beat us," Elenna told him. Stumbling up onto a flat rock, brave Elenna released arrow after arrow towards Nemico. But the boy caught each one as it fell. Tom thought he saw despair in Elenna's eyes. They could not do this alone. Tom felt his own determined spirit being drained by Arax's poisoned spikes. He would need to call upon one of Avantia's good Beasts to help.

Tom raised his sword over his head. "Ferno the fire dragon!" he shouted. "I call on you now!"

Nemico ran towards Tom. "Why don't you just give in?" he mocked, jabbing at Tom with his sword.

"While there's blood in my veins, you won't defeat me," Tom told his enemy.

He felt so weak now, and Nemico was strong. It took all of Tom's remaining energy to fight him.

At last, Tom heard the sound of huge wings beating the air. It was the good Beast Ferno, and he had come to help.

Tom gazed up at Ferno. The dragon dived at the evil boy, surrounding him with flames. Nemico crouched down, using his leather shield as protection until it melted away.

Shocked, he took a few steps backwards, away from the heat, but he was on the very edge of the narrow path. As Nemico teetered on the edge, Tom saw the fear on his face. Even though this boy was his deadly enemy, Tom dived forwards and made a grab for his hand.

But it was too late. With
a howl of despair, Tom's evil
double fell over the edge.

Chapter 2
ARAX RETURNS

Tom looked down. The drop made him feel dizzy, but somehow Nemico was hanging just below the ledge, clinging on by his fingers.

"Help!" Nemico whispered. "Help me...please."

"Let him fall, Tom," he heard Elenna say. Ferno circled above them, snorting in agreement.

But Tom knew he couldn't let

Nemico die. He reached out to grasp the boy's sleeve.

Nemico smiled up at Tom, but for once his eyes didn't have their usual evil glint. His hand slipped through Tom's as if it wasn't there, and he vanished in a cloud of smoke.

"What's happening?" gasped
Tom as the smoke whirled
around him. Gradually the
clouds became a thin spiral
that shot into his body through
the wound left by Arax's

whip. At first Tom felt as if his heart was going to burst, but then he felt...wonderful! His old feelings of strength and determination were returning.

"Tom!" said Elenna, running up to him. "Are you all right?"

"I'm fine," Tom told her. "Everything Arax stole from me has come back. Something must have happened when I took Nemico's hand. I made the right choice when I tried to save him."

A sharp shriek came from
the air above Tom and Elenna.
They could feel the beating of
huge wings as the giant bat
flew right over their heads.

"Watch out!" yelled Elenna, as the Beast swooped towards Tom.

Whoosh! Ferno came diving down towards Arax, unleashing a blast of fire. But Arax was not defeated. He still had his whip, which he flicked straight at Ferno. The fire dragon bellowed and took to the air, avoiding Arax's evil barbs.

"Thank you for helping us, Ferno," Tom shouted up into the air. "It's up to me now. I must finish this Quest!"

Chapter 3
IN THE AIR

With his power restored, Tom knew he was ready for anything. Ferno seemed to understand, and flew away.

With his weapons ready, Tom turned to face his enemy.

Slowly, the Beast began to advance, flicking his evil whip. Just as Arax reached him, Tom swung his shield up. It clashed with the Beast's horns and one

horn sank deep into the shield.
Arax shrieked madly, trying to
shake himself free.

"For Aduro!" Tom yelled. He
brought his sword down on the
other horn and sliced it off.

Arax stumbled about wildly. He managed to shake off the shield but there was no time for Tom to pick it up.

I know the best place to be to avoid Arax's whip, Tom thought, as he jumped onto a rock and leapt high in the air towards Arax's back.

The giant bat snarled with rage as he tried and failed to use his whip against Tom.

Tom raised his sword, but Arax wasn't beaten yet. As the Beast took flight, Tom felt

a great lurch. He could do
nothing but cling on tightly
as Arax sped through the
mountain air.

Higher and higher Tom and Arax flew. Tom could see Elenna far below.

The air around grew icy cold as the giant bat swooped this way and that, until finally Arax shot upwards into the thick grey cloud with Tom on its back.

Swiftly, Tom raised his sword and struck Arax hard over the head. The giant bat cried out in pain and dropped from the sky.

Crash! Arax and Tom fell heavily onto a mountain ledge.

The landing was hard and Tom could hardly breathe. Through his pain, he heard Elenna running towards him.

"Tom! Are you all right?" she cried desperately.

"Don't worry," Tom called back. He knew he'd been lucky. Arax had taken the force of the fall. But Tom could feel the Beast begin to heave

himself up beneath him.

Tom desperately tried to scramble away but he was caught in the giant bat's wings. Then he heard a noise that terrified him. Arax's whip was slicing through the air. The Beast might be hurt, but he was still lashing out.

With all his strength, Tom pushed out his arms and kicked with his legs. The sudden movement knocked Arax off balance, and the whip was flung from the Beast's claws.

Chapter 4
THE FINAL FIGHT

Desperately, Tom threw his head to one side to avoid the whip. The leather cord snaked

past him and sank its spikes
into the Beast's own heart.
With a roar of despair, Arax
flung his wings wide – Tom
was free! The Beast let out a
wail of fear and pain as he
tried to pull the whip from
his chest.

Elenna ran to Tom's side and
they watched as a cloud of
smoke burst from Arax's chest.
The smoke twisted and turned
then broke apart into thin
strands, glowing with every
colour of the rainbow.

"They must be all the souls Arax has stolen," whispered Tom as the strands blew away.

"Do you think the souls are going back to their owners?" asked Elenna.

Tom nodded. "I'm counting on it if Aduro is to be saved," he said.

Tom ran to find his sword and shield from among the rocks, and strode forwards. "Now it's time to finish off this evil Beast for ever," he said.

But something was happening. All over his body, Arax's leathery skin was curling up like paper in a fire. He was turning into dust before Tom and Elenna's astonished eyes!

A sudden wind blew up
and whipped the dust into a
whirlwind. Tom thought he
heard a faint cry of fury as the
cloud was blown high over the
tops of the mountains.

"You did it, Tom!" yelled Elenna. "You defeated Arax!"

"I've never been so happy to be alive!" Tom said, smiling.

They climbed down the path to where Silver and Storm were waiting patiently. The stallion gave a whinny of welcome. Then the air shimmered and a vision of Aduro appeared.

"I thank you both, Tom and Elenna," the good wizard said. "You have rescued me from a terrible torment."

Tom looked hard at the vision of the wizard. "You seem very tired," he said. "Will you recover from this?"

"In time," Aduro replied. His face was still pale, but he smiled. He raised his staff to Tom and Elenna. "Farewell!"

And he was gone.

"Let's go back to the palace for breakfast!" said Tom happily.

Silver ran along barking in delight and Storm trotted ahead. Tom looked at his friend Elenna and smiled. How

could he ever fail with such

companions at his side?

He raised his sword to the sky.

"To our next Quest!" Tom cried.

If you enjoyed this story, you may want to read

Vedra and Krimon
Twin Beasts of Avantia
EARLY READER

Here's how the story begins...

At the Royal Palace of Avantia a birthday party for King Hugo was taking place. As Tom and his friend Elenna raised their glasses in a toast, Elenna whispered in Tom's ear, "Here's to the six beasts of Avantia!"

"Shhh!" warned Tom. Most people believed the Beasts that protected the land were only a legend. But Tom and Elenna had seen them, and freed them from Malvel, an evil wizard.

The good wizard Aduro led the friends away from the party and spoke solemnly to them.

"Two new Beasts have been created," said Aduro. "They are twin dragons, and their names are Vedra and Krimon."

"Baby dragons!" gasped

Elenna, excited. But Aduro was not smiling.

"Their birth could put Avantia in danger," he said, and conjured an image on the wall. It showed the two dragons sleeping in a dark cave. One was green and the other red. Tom and Elenna gazed at the dragons, enchanted.

"Vedra is green and Krimon red," began Aduro as the vision faded. "It is rare for two Beasts to be created together. If Malvel hears about the twins, he will use them for evil purposes and harm Avantia. Will you help to protect the dragons and stop Malvel?"

"Of course we will!" promised Tom and Elenna.

READ

TO FIND OUT WHAT HAPPENS NEXT!

LEARN TO READ WITH

EARLY READER

Beast Quest Early Readers are easy-to-read versions of the original books

Perfect for parents to read aloud and for newly confident readers to read along

Remember to enjoy reading together. It's never too early to share a story!

Series 1
COLLECT THEM ALL!

Meet Tom, Elenna and the
first six Beasts!

TOP THUMPS
COLLECTOR
CARDS INSIDE!
FREE

978-1-84616-483-5

978-1-84616-482-8

978-1-84616-484-2

978-1-84616-486-6

978-1-84616-485-9

978-1-84616-487-3

CONGRATULATIONS, YOU HAVE COMPLETED THIS QUEST!

At the end of each chapter you were awarded a special gold coin. The QUEST in this book was worth an amazing **8** coins.

Look at the Beast Quest totem picture inside the back cover of this book to see how far you've come in your journey to become

MASTER OF THE BEASTS.

The more books you read, the more coins you will collect!

Do you want your own Beast Quest Totem?

1. Cut out and collect the coin below
2. Go to the Beast Quest website
3. Download and print out your totem
4. Add your coin to the totem

www.beastquest.co.uk/totem